FUNNYBONES
A Brilliant Bone-rattling Collection!

Allan Ahlberg & André Amstutz

PUFFIN

PUFFIN BOOKS
Published by the Penguin Group: London, New York, Australia,
Canada, India, Ireland, New Zealand and South Africa
Penguin Books Ltd, Registered Offices: 80 Strand, London WC2R 0RL, England

puffinbooks.com

The Ghost Train first published by William Heinemann Ltd 1992; published in Puffin Books 2006
Bumps in the Night first published by William Heinemann Ltd 1993; published in Puffin Books 2005
Skeleton Crew first published by William Heinemann Ltd 1992; published in Puffin Books 2005
This collection published 2010
012

Text copyright © Allan Ahlberg, 1992, 1993
Illustrations copyright © André Amstutz, 1992, 1993

Made and printed in China

ISBN: 978–0–141–33357–1

CONTENTS

The Ghost Train

ALLAN AHLBERG • ANDRÉ AMSTUTZ

On a dark dark hill
there is a dark dark town.
In the dark dark town
there is a dark dark street.
Down the dark dark street
there is a dark dark station.
And in the dark dark station . . .

there is a ghost train!

Whooooooo!

One night, the big skeleton,
the little skeleton
and the dog skeleton
go for a ride on the ghost train.

They leave the dark dark cellar
and walk down the dark dark street.
They peep in at a few windows
on the way.

"How peaceful!" says the big skeleton.
"How nice!" the little skeleton says.

At the station
they get their tickets
from a monster
and have them punched
by another monster.
"How helpful!" says the big skeleton.
"How kind!" the little skeleton says.

At midnight, the ghost train arrives.
"Do you believe in ghosts?"
says the ghost.
"Yes!" the skeletons say.
"Good," says the ghost.
"Climb aboard!"

And off they go –
out of the dark dark station,
out of the dark dark town,
up and over the dark dark hill
and into the dark dark night.

The ghostly train goes into the night
With a Whoooooo!
The ghostly train goes into the night
With a Whoooooo!
The ghostly train goes into the night,
What a charming sound,
What a peaceful sight,
With a Whoo-ooo-ooo-ooo-ooo!

The three skeletons
sit next to a big monster
and share a joke
with a little monster.
"How friendly!" says the big skeleton.
"What fun!" the little skeleton says.

At one o'clock the train arrives
at Ghost-Town-by-the-Sea.

The skeletons leave the train
and stroll around.
They kick the ghost of a ball
and catch the ghost of a fish.
They paddle in the dark dark sea
and ride on the dark dark donkeys.

THE MONSTERS' BEAUTY PARADE.

"How charming!" says the big skeleton.
"What glamour!" the little skeleton says.

At three o'clock
the ghost train whistle blows.
It is time to leave.
The skeletons climb aboard
and off they go –
away from the dark dark sea,
away from the dark dark sand,
in and out of the *very* dark dark tunnel
and into the dark dark night.

At four o'clock
the train arrives at the station.

The big skeleton, the little skeleton
and the dog skeleton hurry home.
They peep in at a few windows
on the way.
Suddenly, a *baby* cries.
(Do you believe in babies?)
"Waaaaa!"

"How frightful!" says the big skeleton.
"How scary!" the little skeleton says.
"How–l!" howls the dog.

And off they run –
into the house,
down the stairs,
into the cellar
and *under* the bed.

On a dark dark hill
there is a dark dark town.
In the dark dark town
there is a dark dark street.
Down the dark dark street
there is a dark dark station.
And in the dark dark station
there is a ghost train.

Would *you* like a ride?

The End

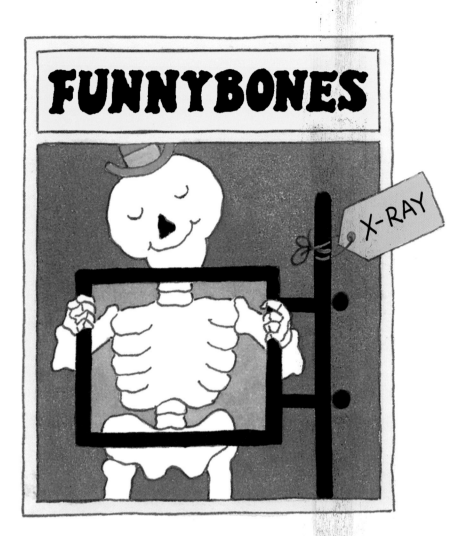

Bumps in the Night

ALLAN AHLBERG • ANDRÉ AMSTUTZ

In the dark dark cellar
of a dark dark house,
a little skeleton is reading a comic.
In the dark dark street
of a dark dark town,
a big skeleton is walking the dog.

Then the big one hurries home,
and the little one hurries out,
and – "Help!" –
they go bump in the night.

In the dark dark classroom
of a dark dark Night School,
a little skeleton is painting a picture.
In the dark dark workshop
of the same Night School,
a big skeleton is making a chair.

Then the little one takes his picture
to show the big one,
and the big one takes his chair
to show the little one,
and – "Wow!" –
they go bump in the night again.

"Send for Doctor Bones!"

The little skeleton and the big skeleton
walk *carefully* to the park.
They swing on the swings,
throw a stick for the dog
and play football.

"The leg bone's connected to the foot bone,"
the little one sings.
"The foot bone's connected to the ball."

The little skeleton and
the big skeleton sit
– but not too close together –
in the dark dark cellar.
"This is a dark dark cellar,"
says the little one. "Let's paint it."
"Good idea!" the big one says.

The big skeleton
and the little skeleton
paint the cellar
and, now and then, the dog.

They paint the cellar
red and green and blue,
and lots more colours.

But . . .
"It's still dark,"
the little skeleton says.
"Let's paint it white."
So, they paint it white . . .

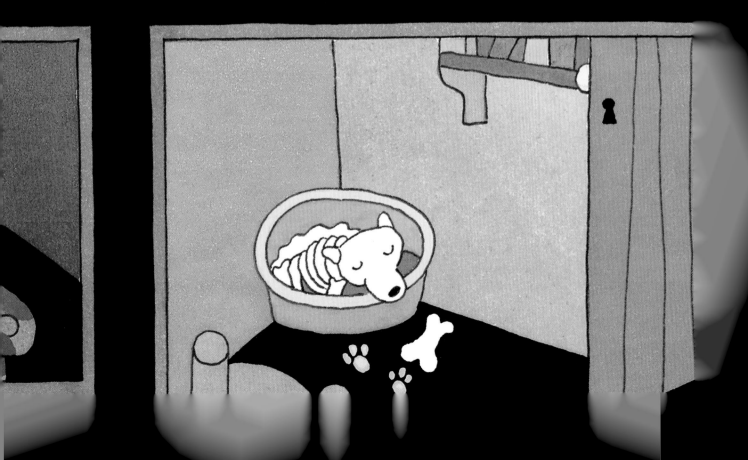

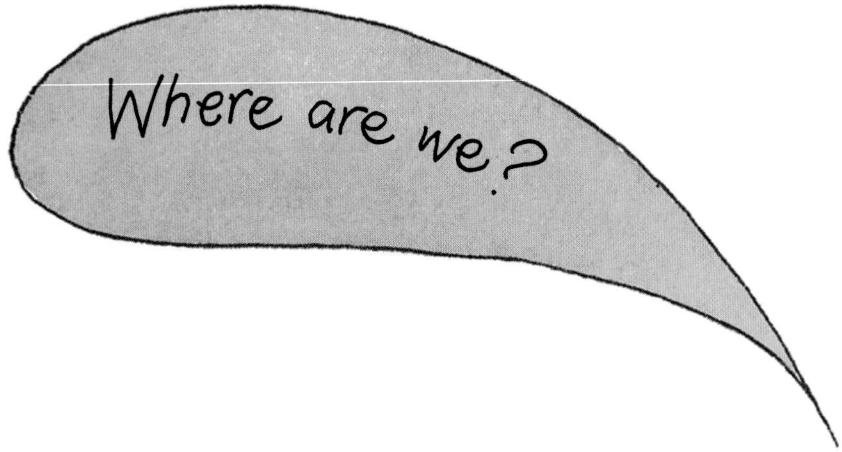
Where are we?

and disappear!
And – you guessed it –
go bump in the night.

"Send for Doctor Bones!"

After that . . .
they go bump in the night playing tennis
and bump in the night playing golf.

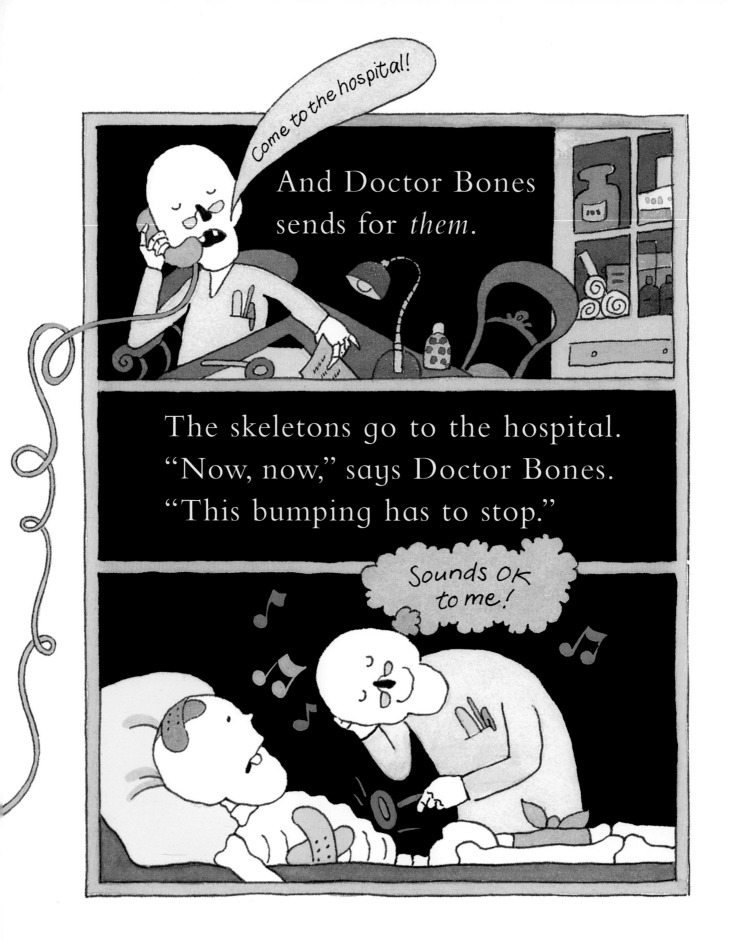

In the dark dark cellar
(they painted it black again)
of a dark dark house,
a little skeleton is fast asleep.
"Zzz!"
In the same cellar of the same house,
a big skeleton is fast asleep too.
"Zzz!"

There they are . . .
tucked up snug and safe at last
from bumps in the night.

Well, nearly.

The End

Skeleton Crew

ALLAN AHLBERG • ANDRÉ AMSTUTZ

On a dark dark night,
on a dark dark sea,
in a dark dark boat
three skeletons float . . .

on a holiday.

The big one is dozing
in his deckchair.
"Zzz!"

The dog one is dozing
in his hammock.
"Zzz!"
The little one is fishing.

. . . and it throws *him* back.

Splash!

The next night
in the dark boat
under the starry sky
the big one has a try.

The big skeleton catches a little fish
and throws it back.
He catches a big fish and keeps it.
He catches a bigger fish . . .

And – "Yo – ho – ho!" –
the *pirates* come.

The pirates climb aboard
looking for treasure.
They steal the deckchair
and the hammock.

Bye-bye!

They steal the fishing rod
and the catfish.
"Miaow!"
They steal . . . the boat!

That's a nice rod – I'll have that!

The next night . . .
nothing happens.

But the *next* night,
under a starry sky
and over the deep blue sea,
the skeletons spy . . . a tree.
"Yippee!"

On the island
the big skeleton
finds a parrot.
"Pretty Polly!"

The next night a lot happens.
A storm blows up.
The thunder crashes,
the lightning flashes,
the wind howls
and the dog howls too.
"Howl!"

As quick as a blink
the raft is blown
across the foam . . .

The End (or is it?)

The End